MW01293711

The

Kingdom of the Elves

Astonishing Adventures Around the World

Book 1

The Elves at the North Pole

NEW YORK CONCEPT

Brownies, like fairies and goblins, are imaginary little sprites, who are supposed to delight in harmless pranks and helpful deeds. They work and sport while weary households sleep, and never allow themselves to be seen by mortal eyes.

Enjoy free episodes at

nyc-books.com

Episode 1
A Dream of Eternal Ice

In the deep woods of the far North, under feathery leaves of fern, was a great fairyland of merry elves, sometimes called forest brownies.

These elves lived joyfully. They had everything at hand and did not need to worry much about living. Berries and nuts grew plentiful in the forest. Rivers and springs provided the elves with crystal water. Flowers prepared them drink from their flavorful juices, which the munchkins loved greatly.

At midnight the elves climbed into flower cups and drank drops of their sweet water with much delight. Every elf would tell a wonderful fairy tale to the flower to thank it for the treat.

Despite this abundance, the pixies did not sit back and do nothing. They tinkered with their tasks all day long. They cleaned their houses. They swung on tree branches and swam in forested streams. Together with the early birds, they welcomed the sunrise, listened to the thunder growling, the whispering of leaves and blades of grass, and the conversations of the animals.

The birds told them about warm countries, sunbeams whispered of distant seas, and the moon spoke of treasures hidden deeply in the earth.

In winter, the elves lived in abandoned nests and hollows. Every sunny day they came out of their burrows and made the forest ring with their happy shouts, throwing tiny snowballs in all directions and building snowmen as small as the pinky finger of a little girl. The munchkins thought they were giants five times as large as them.

With the first breath of spring, the elves left their winter residences and moved to the cups of the snowdrop flowers. Looking around, they watched the snow as it turned black and melted. They kept an eye on the blossoming of hazel trees while the leaves were still sleeping in their warm buds. They observed squirrels moving their last winter supplies from storage back to their homes. Gnomes welcomed the birds coming back to their old nests, where the elves lived during winters. Little by little, the forest once more grew green.

One moonlight night, elves were sitting at an old willow tree and listening to mermaids singing about their underwater kingdom.

"Brothers! Where is Murzilka? He has not been around for a long time!" said one of the elves, Father Beardie, who had a long white beard. He was older than others and well respected in his striped stocking cap.

"I'm here," a snotty voice arose, and Murzilka himself, nicknamed Feather

Head, jumped from the top of the tree. All the brothers loved Murzilka, but thought he was lazy, as he actually was. Also, he loved to dress in a tailcoat, tall black hat, boots with narrow toes, a cane and a single eyeglass, being very proud of that look.

"Do you know where I'm coming from? The very Arctic Ocean!" roared he.

Usually, his words were hard to believe. That time, though, his announcement sounded so marvelous that all elves around him were agape with wonder.

"You were there, really? Were you? How did you get there?" asked the sprites.

"As easy as ABC! I came by the fox one day and caught her packing her things to visit her cousin, a silver fox who lives by the Arctic Ocean.

"Take me with you," I said to the fox.

"Oh, no, you'll freeze there! You know, it's cold there!" she said.

"Come on." I said. "What are you talking about? What cold? Summer is here."

"Here we have summer, but there they have winter," she answered.

"No," I thought. "She must be lying because she does not want to give me a ride."

Without telling her a word, I jumped upon her back and hid in her bushy fur, so even Father Frost could not find me.

Like it or not, she had to take me with her.

We ran for a long time. Another forest followed our woods, and then a boundless plain opened, a swamp covered with lichen and moss. Despite the intense heat, it had not entirely thawed.

"This is tundra," said my fellow traveler.

"Tundra? What is tundra?" asked I.

"Tundra is a huge, forever frozen wetland covering the entire coast of the Arctic Ocean. It means we are not that far from my cousin."

Indeed, soon we stopped at a burrow which smelled of rotten fish and other decay.

"What a wonderful smell, isn't it?" said my fox. "You can tell a rich girl lives here!" Our hostess flew out of the hole as soon as she heard our voices and immediately fell upon her cousin's neck in welcome.

She was so happy that she did not know where to seat us and how to treat us, while her barns burst with plenty. Obviously, she lived in abundance, and the fur she wore was black with silvery shimmering!

We ate, rested and went for a walk along the beach. Brothers, you would not believe what I saw! There were mountains glistening in the sun like diamonds, swept by the waves. Continents, islands, castles and rocks sailed behind them, and polar bears and other sea monsters were sitting on them. All of it was made from clear crystal ice which shone and glinted under the sun!

The elves could not believe in what they just heard. How could they not know about such extraordinary miracles?

"Whoopee, we shall visit this eternal ice, this snow and this ocean!" raised the voices. "Why should we stay in one place?"

"Vote for me as your leader!" shouted Murzilka, "I know the way—."

"No!" his brothers interrupted him. "You are too frivolous. We vote for Uncle Harelip. He is steady and serious. He would not give us bad advice!"

"Hooray, Uncle Harelip! Hoooray!" shouted the elves, throwing up their round caps of invisibility.

Uncle Harelip, chosen as the guide, was a plump old man who wore a cap with a big peak in summer and winter. His upper-lip was covered with a gray mustache and was pushed out. That is why he was called Harelip.

"To undertake such a long journey, we must prepare very well," said Uncle Harelip. "I think we cannot hit the road before the first snowfall. By that time we will have everything ready."

The same night, uncle went to the Forest Witch to get some fern blossom.

"Where are you going?" wondered she.

"To see the world, to show ourselves," answered the elf, "you know, there are all kinds of dangers on the road. So, I'd like to get the fern blossom for all of us to turn invisible in case."

"It is good to be cautious," noted the Forest Witch. "Here is a whole batch for you, enough for everybody."

The elf thanked her, took the gift on his back, and went further to meet the mermaid Marenka.

Marenka had just left her amber castle and come ashore. She sat on a branch of a weeping willow tree, and under the light of the moon, sorted the unearthly treasures that sparkled in her transparent hands. The little mermaid laughed loudly with pleasure and swayed the willow.

"Good night, Marenka! I came to you for the sponge boots that do not burn in fire and do not sink in water," explained the brownie.

"Hahaha!" laughed the mermaid. "I know, I know: You want to travel. Fish told me about that. Please, catch it!" She threw a sack full of tiniest boots down the tree.

Saying "Thank you," Uncle Harelip shouldered the bundle and went to is home under the fern.

In busy tasks, the summer flew away. With the first snow in the woods, axes and hammers chattered. Sprites tore chunks of bark from birch trees, flattened them, inserted sticks, and made marvelous sleds like snow scooters. The Little People were satisfied with their work and could not wait to embark on the road.

"Hoo-hoo-hoo", cheeped baby owls on a tree. "The Forest People are going somewhere! Hoohooo! They will not play with us any longer during winter evenings. Hoohoo! We will tell about it to mammy, hoo!"

When the owlets woke the next morning, they did not see the elves. They had left the same night on a glassy snow road to the great Arctic Ocean.

Episode 2

The Elves at the North Pole

On the day when the first snow fell, early in the daybreak, the elves set out for the Arctic Ocean. Their snow scooters merrily flew, driven by this frisky fellowship, and the pixies laughed loudly. Their eyes were glowing with glee at sliding through the snow. Each one tried to shout louder than the others, but Murzilka screamed the loudest:

"Am I an attaboy?! Look at me. I am handsome! I am a dandy!"

Suddenly there was a crash and a cry, and the elves sitting on the front sleighs looked back with fear. Oh! They shouted. How terrible! The rear sled had flown into a tree and fallen in halves. Everybody dug into the soft snow.

Their brothers immediately began to pull out the poor fellows from the snow banks. Soon everybody was out except Murzilka. Though hundreds of tiny hands were digging into the snow piles, it took a while before they saw two legs sticking up. The elves grabbed them all together and drew the boy out.

A great sad face had Murzilka when he shook off the snow. He was red and wrinkled like a baked apple. His hands trembled, the collar of his coat stuck to his skinny body, the monocle fell, and his hat was broken. Murzilka looked so pathetic and ridiculous that the sprites, in spite of their pity, laughed loudly.

"Why are you laughing?" asked Murzilka proudly. "Instead of laughing, you'd better praise me for bravery!"

"Bravery? Why?" almost unanimously asked the elves.

"Why indeed? Didn't you see?" angrily asked Murzilka. "As soon as our slide bumped up against the tree, I was the first one who foresaw the danger and jumped out into the snow."

"Don't you lie, please." said suddenly one elf in a thin voice. "I sat beside you, and like me, you were just thrown out of the sleigh. You, Murzilka, were just pushed out unwillingly."

Having quickly fixed the snow scooter, the elves continued their journey.

Soon ended the forest, to be followed by the boundless tundra. On the way, the pixies often came across wolves, polar bears, and silver foxes. They met Nenets

people in narrow sleds, carried by Samoeyd dogs, and the herds of deer looking for moss under the snow. The further they went, the more deserted and vast the tundra became. The land was covered with clouds and fog. The excellent elves' ears heard icebergs crashing and colliding in the distance.

Murzilka had calmed down and was loud again, singing and shouting praises for himself.

The tundra ended as well, and the little people pushed on into the kingdom of the snow, frost, night, and ice. They were welcomed by tiny snowflakes like girls with starred and four-cornered crystal dresses.

The girl-snowflakes hosted the travelers and showed them the route.

The snow was everywhere, and the elves did not even know whether they were on the coast or on the ocean because the dark, impenetrable night surrounded them. Great stars gleamed distant in the sky.

The brownies did not know what to do, and even Murzilka got quiet. Suddenly, though, came a great wonder! The sky was covered with the colored circles, each coming from one spot. Every minute they became brighter and brighter. All at once, the whole sky flashed and flamed with splashes of rainbow light, dusting the earth with millions of spatter drops.

The sprites screamed with delight. The snow and ice—everything sparkled and became as bright as on a sunny day. Then, they saw mountains, continents, castles, and caves, all shining like diamonds.

"What is it?" they asked each other.

It was the Northern Lights.

"Brothers!" Murzilka exclaimed. "Look, there are some creatures coming!"

The Little People looked where Murzilka pointed and silently waited.

Great was their joy when they recognized elves like themselves in the newcomers.

The elves rushed toward each other. Murzilka was the first, of course, who noticed the strange outfits of the other pixies. There were five of them: An Eskimo, a Sailor in a blue shirt and a blue hat with an anchor logo on it, a Turk, a Chinese with a long braid, and a Doctor in a high hat and tuxedo.

"How did you get here?" asked our elves in the same breath.

"Oh, don't even ask!" cried the Chinese. "We lived in an evergreen garden, in a pleasant country, without any troubles, when suddenly this schlep (he pointed to the Eskimo) decided to travel. He talked us into doing that! It'd take a while to describe our wandering before we got here. You see what a paradise we live in now! The cold wind blows on and on all winter long. The snow almost buries us. There is no a single soul around except white bears! What a great state!"

"How about people?" asked the Sailor. "People!" the Eskimo yelled. "These poor guys are worse than us. They had not thought about the proper time to sail on a ship. One morning they came out on the deck and found the ocean smooth as a mirror all around. The poor things were in anguish and moved to the shore. They built small igloos from the ice, trampled them hard with snow, and dragged their supplies from the ship. They have been hard at work for three months already.

Their food is at an end, and they can barely stay on their feet from cold and hunger. They are under constant fear of a polar bear, who often visits them. Who knows whether they will endure till the spring!"

The elves wiped tears with their tiny caps, listening to the Eskimo.

"We will help them, certainly we will help!" they squeaked. "Take us to these poor fellows!" And the whole crowd followed the storyteller.

Soon, they reached four square igloos. Each elf stuck a flower of the fern into a buttonhole and became invisible. Though, there were so many of them, they took so little space that even without the flowers of invisibility, they would not have been noticed.

The elves were surprised inside the snow hut because it was almost empty. On a fire in the middle was a boiling pot with some fish, emitting a foul odor. Five people were sitting around it warming their stiff limbs. They were wrapped in buckskin, but the cold penetrated through the fur.

These poor sailors had been caught by a sudden early northern winter. They had to stay in the harsh country for many months. Hunger with its dire consequences waited for them, but luckily, our good elves came.

They settled in the igloos and began to ease the lives of the ice prisoners.

They ran in their fast sponge boots along the shore, tracking down foxes, sables and other beasts, and driving them to the snow huts so that the people would have food.

The sailors were surprised with such a sudden abundance of wildlife.

The igloos became warm and cozy. At times, the people heard "Cied-Cied-Cied." from the corners. Thus spoke the elves, but the people did not know about that and thought that some crickets climbed in through a crack in the wall.

At night, when everybody was sleeping in igloos, the elves came ashore to enjoy the magical view of the northern lights, which were like wonderful fireworks covering half of the sky.

Episode 3
The Elves and the Whale

Six months passed, and the long-lasting winter nights sometimes turned into short, misty, gray dawns which could not even be called days.

On one of these dismal daybreaks, Draggle Tail Sorcerer, who always knew news before anyone else, told the brothers that the night before he had seen a light beam cross the beach and then move beyond. Indeed, it was not long before the sky gradually lightened, the mist brightened, and the first dull rays of sunshine shone through. So began to awaken and shift and stir the dormant, dreaming Northern Wilderness. Again, they heard the ice start to crackle and break. The sun slowly came out, and the fog rose.

Thus awakened the northern spring.

Whole icebergs and small floes floated about with walruses lying on them. The sailors were happy and cheerfully began to fix the ship to go fishing and then to go back home, where they probably had been given up for lost.

Our elves also spent whole days on the beach.

"Brothers!" called Draggle Tail Sorcerer with a voice full of surprise. "Come, come here! A black mountain with a fountain is approaching us!"

The brownies rushed to Draggle Tail Sorcerer and stood stock-still. On the surface of the Arctic Ocean they saw a giant whale. Out of his nostrils rose a high column of water gushing out like a fountain.

"Godzilla!" cried Murzilka. "This is a magnificent ship! Let's take a ride on it, my friends! An opportunity to sail on such a ship knocks only once!"

"Oh, yes, it's a great idea," agreed the others. In an instant, all were shod in the sponge boots that do not burn in fire and do not sink in water and bravely they ran on the thin ice.

The whale could not see our invisible pixies and continued to lie quietly.

Its broad back served as an enormous deck where the lively crowd ran squealing and squeaking. The fact that he danced on the whale's head was not enough for Murzilka, so with his cane he even poked the beast in its nostrils, from which the fountain was leaping.

The giant winced. It obviously felt the uninvited guests, and a high jet from the fountain caught Murzilka's hat and threw it into the ocean.

"My hat! My brand new hat!" cried Murzilka, but the other elves had their own worries.

The whale's tail violently beat on the water, showering the sprites all over from head to toe. The high waves, ready to wash away the helpless brothers, went around them.

The columns of water, each higher than the one before, spouted out of the nostrils of the whale. Its bulky body cut through the waves so quickly that the poor elves thought they were about to fall into the abyss. But then, suddenly—oh, no, no, no!

The whale swiftly plunged deep into the depths. If, luckily for them, there had not been the wreckage of the crushed ship around, which they grabbed desperately, the elves would have died, each and all.

"Help! Help!" shouted Murzilka, who managed to catch his hat on the hop. The hat, however, was all wet, and the water teemed from it. "Don't you see what happened to my hat? How do I wear it now? Well, it has become quite shabby ...."

"Shut up!" the Chinese said to him. "Don't you see that the others do not walk in the woods, but stay silent? Shall we worry now about your hat?!"

Murzilka muttered something to himself that nobody understood and began to wipe his hat carefully with his handkerchief, paying little attention to the dangers which threatened all of them.

Those dangers were really serious. Great logs quickly rushed forward, colliding with ice floes. Unguided by anyone, they floated freely anywhere the flow carried them. The elves watched after each other with fear so nobody would be left behind or fall into the water.

They sailed across the ocean for days and weeks without seeing anything but sky and water. Finally, one morning they noticed that they floated not in the ocean, but in a narrow strait.

"Rejoice, rejoice!" cried the Chinese. "I know this area! If only we can hold to the south and reach the shore, there will be my homeland!"

It took, however, many days of hardship and adversity before the exhausted elves landed.

And so began their adventure in China.

Book 2
From China to India

BROWNIES, like fairies and goblins, are imaginary little sprites, who are supposed to delight in harmless pranks and helpful deeds. They work and sport while weary households sleep, and never allow themselves to be seen by mortal eyes.

Episode 4
Fishing in China

The mountainous coast where our elves landed was covered with a rich vegetation the sprites had never seen. Tall, slender palm trees grew mixed with almond and orange trees. Large bright flowers gleamed with all sorts of colors. Shiny birds filled the air with wondrous singing. Butterflies three times larger than the tallest elf flew from one flower cup to another, sparkling in the sun with their marvelous wings.

The brownies rushed to the soft grass with pleasure and began to feast on flower dust.

Suddenly, the squeaky voice of Draggle Tail Sorcerer was sounded.

"Friends, look up! There is somebody sitting there!"

The surprised gnomes leaped to their feet and saw many tiny elves like themselves, but with bright wings on their back, sitting on the low, overhanging dark green branches. Those elves were looking at the strangers with both fear and curiosity.

"Don't be afraid, my friends!" said Uncle Harelip, calling to the winged elves. "We will not do any harm to you, but we do need your help!"

"Oh, in that case, we are delighted to see you!" rang the voices from the branch. "Welcome! Climb up here to our heights!"

In a moment, so many elves climbed up to the branch that it crashed and fell down into the soft moss, where Murzilka and the Chinese, whose actual name was Chi-ka-chi, were sitting next to each other.

Chi-ka-chi deftly climbed out in an instant, but the other elves had to drag out Murzilka, a coward who was a half dead with fear, although he was not hurt. He still screamed and cried in a loud voice.

Having recovered from their fright, the elves sat around an old stump and began to talk to each other about their living.

"Oh, what the heroes you are!" exclaimed the winged elves, listening to the story of the guests. "You probably know that you are now in China, a country where tea grows?"

"In my country!" added Chi-ka-chi. "Oh, yeah! You bet, I was the first who knew it was our China. Now we are going to the city. I want to show to all my friends what beautiful people live here."

So they decided to go to a nearby town at dawn.

As soon as the first rays of the sun came out, the sprites jumped out of their green beds and ran for all they were worth towards the town. The sponge boots lifted them like lightning, and they entered the city very early.

Despite the early hour, crowds of people scurried about the narrow streets. There were sellers of various products, boys with swallows' nests and worms, which the Chinese find wonderful food, and officials who rushed about doing their duties. One- and two-story houses decorated with intricate carvings and awnings stood on both sides of the street. All the roofs were connected with each other by walkways, creating a high street with the same busy motion as the lower one.

The elves climbed up. There they could see the whole city, with its towers and pagodas or temples.

The pixies ran like blazes in the direction through the city, where they noticed the Chinese gods. With each hour, the streets became more crowded.

The sedan chairs with noble ladies, Chinese dignitaries, appeared. The ladies were dressed in motley clothing, with high hairstyles which held bird cages and bouquets of flowers. The men had dangling braids. The more important the man was, the longer he wore his braid: Barons had them all the way to their toes.

They, as well as women, were dressed up, but instead of a high hairstyle, they wore hats with loads of golden beads and bells. Upon meeting, the barons bowed to each other for a long time, bending and squatting.

The elves scattered around the city, looking closely at the characteristics of the Chinese culture. When they came together in the evening at the appointed place, each in turn told how he spent the day and what he saw and learned. The stories were very interesting, and the conversation lasted past midnight.

Uncle Harelip and Father Beardie told how they wandered around the neighborhood. They enthusiastically reported that Chinamen were hardworking and patient. They loved to toil thoughtfully around their homes, especially in their tea gardens, which one could see at almost every village house. Turk said that so many people were in China that they did not have enough land for everybody, so many were forced to live on the rivers, arranging rafts for themselves. These hard-working Chinese people brought black earth aboard their rafts, so they had houses with floating, flowery gardens and backyards.

Draggle Tail Sorcerer loudly told how he visited the house of a baron and watched him drawing a portrait of his wife with a mercury ink.

Only Murzilka, the Feather Head, could not tell anything good because all day long he just ran through the streets and pulled the braids of the Chinese.

The elves liked living in China, and they decided to stay longer in the country.

One day they went to the beach. It was still very early. The boats were sliding on the smooth surface of the water. In each of them sat a Chinese with a few birds. The birds in turn dived into the water and pulled out fish each time. The munchkins got excited about such fishing, but how could they arrange it without trained birds?

The fish, as ill luck would have it, were jumping and playing on the surface, teasing the elves.

"Fellows, I know how to solve our problem!" said Dr. Ointment, wearing a tall hat and a tuxedo with long, narrow tails. "I saw many times how they catch these dancing fish. We just need to fashion fishing rods ...."

"Let's go!" said the elves.

In seconds some ran to the swamp for reeds; others hurried to the city for hooks and thread; and the last ones went digging for worms. The Turk brought the buckets, boxes, and the shovels from the forest, and the bunch of them began to work.

The flexible canes were soon falling under the elves' sharp knives, and the boxes were bustling with insects. Soon, the thread and hooks were on hand as well. The elves were busy at beginning to work, but there was a shriek and howl from Murzilka.

As always, instead of helping his brothers, his disasters delayed them. He opened the boxes and began to count the worms to find out who had caught the most of them.

Suddenly, from one of the boxes flew a flock of mosquitoes which painfully bit Murzilka. The poor elf ran away, but it did not help: The mosquitoes chased him, buzzing angrily.

They would have bitten poor Murzilka badly, but his busy brothers defended him from the furious creatures. While the elves were fiddling with moaning Murzilka, the sun passed into the afternoon, and the fish fled into hiding. The brownies found nothing to do but put off the fishing until the next fine morning.

Early in the morning the next day, they threw their rods. What a joy! The fat fish just jumped at the bait.

Draggle Tail Sorcerer was the first who pulled in an outlandish fish. Then Hairlip and Bear Squeaker almost caught an eel, which deftly wiggled through their hands. They tried to take it by the tail, but it slipped into the water, almost taking them with it.

Murzilka, meanwhile, paced up and down among his working brothers whistling a merry tune. He, as usual, interfered with everything, and, among other things, sat down at the water and began to splash it out in all directions. Suddenly, he lost his balance and fell into the flowing stream. If it were not Dr. Ointment and other fellows who grabbed Murzilka, he would probably have drowned.

The forest folk lived fine and freely in China. Nobody disturbed them or hindered their amusements. The little men came up with many different fun activities.

Among other things, to celebrate the successful fishing day during which Murzilka almost lost his life, the elves decided to fly their kites.

Episode 5

The Kites and the Boats

The Chinese elf Chi-ka-chi was a great master of kite-building and a talented artist at painting them. To get the right material, the pixies sent messengers to the city. Since our invisible friends needed very little, they could easily get everything they needed. The most important commission was given to Draggle Tail Sorcerer: He was instructed to get the flour required to prepare a glue. Artful Draggle Tail Sorcerer soon returned with a sack of flour, but in hurry he did not notice that the bag was untied, and half of the flour had scattered on the road.

Meanwhile, Bear Squeaker went for the paper. To find it, he had to get to the rich baron's house since he knew they had long, thin sheets of paper there. The baron's house was surrounded by a triple-walled fence with gates and towers. Behind it stretched a large courtyard, in the middle of which stood the elaborate house of the important baron. Bear Squeaker had no trouble climbing through the fences and penetrating into the rooms, the glitter and luxury of which struck the elf.

In some rooms, between the roses and greenery, he found fragrant fountains; in others, the walls, floor and ceiling had rare paintings; in the third ones, the walls were covered with gold and silver decorations. The sprite quietly went to the library of the host, where he hoped to find the right things. He had to go through the dining room, where the family had just gathered for dinner.

"Let's see what the rich make a feast of," thought the elf.

He jumped onto the table and sat down in a vase of flowers. To the great surprise of Bear Squeaker, the dinner began with the desert and ended with the bread and boiled rice.

"Funny people! Everything they do is topsy-turvy," thought Bear Squeaker, jumping out of his ambush. "But I have to hurry!" So, he grabbed two packs of paper and ran like lightning back home right on time, since everybody had been waiting for him and the Eskimo, who was searching for thin, light sticks.

The Eskimo was also late. He thought that he would get the wands in the forest near the tea garden. When he came there, though, the sprigs of the tea trees were kept so neat and clean that he was reluctant to break them. Therefore, the Eskimo decided to go to a nearby garden. Again, there was the same amazingly clean and tidy order. Willy-nilly, he had to climb into the garden of a baron. "At least, even if I ruin something, they would not lose much," thought the elf.

Finding himself among exuberant vegetation of the baron's garden, the sprite was delighted. The pathways were strewn with colored stones and shells, and intricate caves and gazebos were hiding in the midst of flowers.

When the Eskimo, panting, hurried home with his catch, the work was humming.

Snappy tied corn tassels to make the tail of the kites. Quick Footed lugged water. Doono and Dunno were cooking the paste, and burned each other's hands with boiling water several times.

In a word, the work was in full swing. One kite followed another. The Chinese elf was painting the most detailed decorations on them, to the total delight of the crowd.

As soon as the sun reached the East, the elves left their floral forest beds and plunged out with their kites on the large spacious meadow. At a signal, dozens of dainty kites were released and easily lifted into the air.

"Yay! Yay!" shouted the elves in unison, raising their tiny heads up and carefully following the flight of the kites.

Suddenly, they heard someone desperately crying and squeaking.

The elves could not get what was going on, but thought the squeaking might be birds tangled in the thin strings.

"Help! Save me! Help!" rang a shrill voice that the elves soon realized belonged to Murzilka.

Fearing the worst, the sprites left their kites and rushed to their ill-fated companion.

He had managed to tangle his feet in the ties and turned upside down. While they ran to help, Murzilka, to everyone's consternation, lifted up with the kites to a dizzy height. They managed to release him with a great difficulty.

The thin ropes deeply dug into Murzilka's legs, and even after he was released, he continued to moan desperately.

Fortunately, Dr. Ointment always had different medications ready in the long tails of his coat and immediately smeared Murzilka's sore spots with some mixture so that the pain soon passed.

For a long while after that, until the sun went down, the elves played with their kites.

The days and weeks passed, and finally the elves grew bored in China and wanted to go further to unknown lands. Only how could they escape all difficulties of their previous trip?

At that time along the shore where our forest people sat, small sailing boats were floating by.

"That would be useful for our trip!" thought Draggle Tail Sorcerer and secretly disappeared. No one knew where he was hiding.

On the third day, at midnight, he appeared before the brothers and mysteriously announced that he knew where there was a large warehouse of boats, namely those they had seen recently

The elves were delighted with the discovery, and the same night they followed Draggle Tail Sorcerer to the nearby seaside town.

Soon they came to a huge building in which, as indicated by the sorcerer, the boats were stored. The little ones, without hesitation, went inside through the cracks in the walls and the keyholes, opened out the doors with a magic bust-grass, picked out some nice boats and floated them out, shouting and singing. They tucked away the boats in the dense reeds and then, as if nothing had happened, went back into the forest, planning to embark on another long journey the next midnight.

The day passed in fuss and foolery. They had to prepare one thing after another to take, cook for the road, and settle who would go with whom and where to go.

Gradually the evening came. The moon glowed in all its glory, shining through the southern sky and shading the forests and fields in its blue, flickering light. The greater stars shimmered and glimmered in the sky. The fragrant breezes softly breathed on the sleepy land, going up and down.

The elves said farewell to their hospitable hosts, took their seats in the boats, and bravely embarked on a calm sea.

For many days they rode in their light, invisible shells through different seas: The Yellow, Blue and China Seas passed behind them.

The journey went well. Only once did the pixies pass a peril, accidentally hitting underwater rocks.

The boats sprung leaks, but thanks to the skills and agility of Harelip, the elves avoided the danger. Having fixed the boats at the nearest land, these forest folk went back on their watery road the next day.

The sea was like an azure valley, gently lulling, but sometimes it grew great waves and tossed towering spray from its gray ridges.

Still the sprites sailed forward. They desired to see a dreamland, often told of by Draggle Tail Sorcerer and Dr. Ointment. It was India, the country they had dreamed of in the far north, among the cold and frost. Now, skirting the coasts of the islands and the mainland, the elves rushed into that magical land.

Episode 6
The Elves in India

One morning Murzilka arose to a great surprise when an elf named Topsy-Turvy woke him to wonder if he would like to see a huge Indian elephant, on which a son of the Raja soon would take a walk.

Murzilka opened his eyes and slowly squinted around.

"Elephant? ... Raja? ... Walk ...?" he asked his friend. "Where are we now? Aren't we sailing on the sea?"

"Wow, my friend, you seemed to sink into a deep sleep on the journey and did not notice how we landed on the shores of India and carried you still snoozing away here into this palace of the Indian Raja," explained Topsy-Turvy.

"Raja? Tell me truly, please! What is a Raja? I have never heard this word."

"Raja is an Indian prince. We are settled right in the palace of one of these princes. Outsiders are strictly forbidden to enter this place, but we invisible ones can get anywhere."

Murzilka quickly scrambled to his feet and went with his companion through a series of rooms into the garden, where the other elves had been wishing and waiting for the elephant.

The luxury of the palace of this Raja struck Murzilka.

Expensive oriental rugs covered the floors and walls. A domed roof rose on golden pillars studded with sapphires and emeralds, and silver fabric in the form of clouds covered it. Wonderful oriental lanterns made from precious metals hung from the ceiling, and blue vases were full of flowers. Every room smelled sweet, and this aroma soaked all things. On the floor in picturesque disorder lay precious cushions used instead of chairs.

Murzilka really wanted to see every room in detail, but Topsy-Turvy hurried him along hastily, fearing that the elephant might be gone.

Murzilka and his friend went into the garden where all other elves had been waiting, either sitting on the fence or on the ground. There were Dr. Ointment, Draggle Tail Sorcerer, Doono and Dunno. They all listened closely to Quick Footed, who said that Indians used elephants instead of horses.

Before he could even finish the story, a huge white elephant approached the porch. His back and head were covered with an expensive cloth.

The elves at first were afraid to come close to the elephant, but since he was standing quietly, swaying his long trunk, they approached him and began to climb on his back, somersaulting and jumping joyously. Even Dr. Ointment started to jump with the others, and soon the little men made a real circus on the back of the elephant. Only Murzilka stood aside and was afraid to come closer.

"Don't be afraid," shouted Draggle Tail Sorcerer. "The elephant is friendly! It won't harm you!"

"No, no, I am just afraid that it might catch my new hat with its long trunk," replied Murzilka.

"There is nothing to be afraid of," said an elf in a narrow cap and a short jacket, whose name was Dindunduk.

But Murzilka did not let himself to be persuaded.

Soon one of the servants of the Raja, dressed in expensive clothes, climbed the stairs to the elephant, sat between its ears and lightly tapped it, and the elephant, gently stepping, moved onto the path.

When the elephant began to walk, the elves followed it, and together with the elephant ran to the Indian city, close to the palace of the Raja.

All day long, our forest people scuttled around the city, crawling through all keyholes from the luxurious palace to the poorest Indian hut, peering curiously at everything.

"Nice people, these Indians," said Murzilka on the road.

By evening, the sprites gathered again at the palace of the Raja. Coming back, the elves were amazed by unexpected magical views. The whole garden, the house, and the lake were sparkling with thousands of different colored lights blinding everybody around. The greens seemed like a fantastic fabric, and the flowers like magical fairies.

Sniffing among people, the pixies learned that the festival and fireworks were arranged in honor of the Raja.

The elves liked fireworks so much, that they decided to make something like that at the birthday of Draggle Tail Sorcerer.

No sooner said than done: Our invisible brownies waded into the lodge where firecrackers were stored and began to take whole boxes of sparklers, stars, rockets, multi-colored lanterns and other noisemakers, as nobody, of course, could see them.

"Move faster, don't be lazy!" shouted Murzilka, but he, as usual, did not want to work himself, pleading that his hat was in the way.

Grunting and groaning, the elves dragged their load to a small lawn near the palace.

"Wait, wait!" cried again Murzilka, "here it's best to arrange our celebration."

Having placed everything as it should, the elves began to light the fireworks.

Four rockets, hissing and whistling, flew up into the black sky, and a diamond rain fell into the nearest river.

"Yay! Yay!" shouted the elves in unison.

The fireworks began. Huge birds, shields and monograms burned with millions of colors. There were dazzling stars, flowers and whirling sheaves scattering and illuminating the whole area.

Dr. Ointment pulled out more and more new rockets. They made a snake, Roman candles and mushrooms. Each rocket had no time to go out before the new one was firing up.

In the palace, everybody was very surprised with the magical fireworks, and the Raja decided that a miracle had happened.

That night, the elves again went to the palace. They made themselves snug on the carpets and cushions that lay on the floor in all the rooms of the palace. The little ones were very tired and fell asleep so soundly that they woke up only when the servants of the Raja began to shake the carpets in the morning.

Outside on the street, the elves noticed a poorly dressed woman with a child in her arms. She was crying bitterly about something.

"This woman probably belongs to the pariahs, or untouchables," said Dr. Ointment. "Do you know, my friends, who are the pariahs?"

Nobody knew.

"Pariahs," explained the doctor, "are the people who belong to the poorest class in India, outcasts from society for a misconduct. Here in India, they are all shunned and subject to hate, so even beggars despise them. They live separately from the rest of the world, and nobody wants to know them."

"Poor people!" exclaimed in unison our elves.

"Is it possible to help this woman with anything?"

"Let's listen to her complaints," Dr. Ointment said.

From the woman's story, the elves learned that she had a small apiary, but that night someone had robbed her and broken up all the hives.

"Dears, I know how to help this woman!" cried Murzilk, after hearing the story. "Walking through the forest, I distinctly heard the buzzing of bees. They probably hid in a hollow tree. Let's go there and collect them for the poor woman."

Our little people really liked Murzilka's idea, so without thinking twice, they immediately went to the forest. In the place indicated by Murzilka, they found a row of old tamarind trees and, indeed, the buzzing of the bees could be heard as if it came from the underground. They puzzled how to get them.

First, the pixies tried to knock on wood with sticks and stones, but the bees did not come out. Then, having armed themselves with borer, saws, axes and hammers, these brave bee hunters began to expel the stubborn bugs from the hollow and planned to put them all into a prepared beehive.

The work did not go well at first. Quick Footed got a splinter in the eye; Dunno broke his ax in half and hurt his finger at the same time. Pinwheel cut his leg with an ax. Fortunately, he immediately bandaged the wound, so he lost only a little blood.

Murzilka was haughty, pacing back and forth giving orders to the comrades to hurry.

After much effort, the elves noticed the bees in cut holes.

"Yay! Yay!" cried Dr. Ointment, who was the first to notice the bees. "Bring the hive quickly."

The elves placed the hive they had prepared in advance at one of the holes and puttied all other openings. Then, they began to knock on the barrel.

The frightened insects rushed to the exit, and everyone was trapped. The sprites triumphantly carried the hive with the bees tied in a sheet to the hut of the poor woman. An old hollow banana tree grew in front of the doors of the hut, and the little people hoped to hang the hive there.

Our brownies were climbing over the high fence of the village when an unexpected adventure happened. The knot came untied somehow, and a bevy of bees flew out with a buzz. They rushed on the defenseless elves, especially at Murzilka and Father Beardie. The bees stung everywhere on Murzilka's head and face.

With great difficulty, the pixies placed the hive onto a tree. The bees recognized it as their old home and busily began to settle. Just imagine the joy of the woman when she returned home and found the hive! The poor lady cried with joy.

The elves immediately turned invisible and laughed merrily. Only Murzilka was sad, looking at his hands covered with red spots from the bites of the bees.

No matter how well lived the little forest people in the palace of the Indian Raja, they still decided to go somewhere else as soon as possible and waited only for an opportunity to hit the road.

One morning Chinese Chi-ka-chi ran to them, all out of breath, and called everybody, claiming that there was something important to tell them.

The elves immediately surrounded the Chinese, who told them in a loud voice:

"Yesterday when I got into the swallow's nest under the roof, I heard the old swallow tell her neighbor that tomorrow at dawn they will fly with a large company across the sea to distant lands where the spring is coming now. So I thought," added Chi-ka-chi, "what if we sit on the backs of these air travelers and move to another part of the world without worries?"

"There's a dear! Clever boy! Yay!" shouted the elves. "What can be easier and more convenient than such a trip? Long live the Chi-ka-chi!"

They sent Draggle Tail Sorcerer to investigate. After some time, he reported that the swallows would start out at dawn.

The sprites came to the hill where the departure was scheduled and waited.

As soon as a pink strip in the east appeared, the swallows flew over from all directions.

The birds busily rose above the trees, then down to the ground. Finally, they formed a great black cluster and quickly soared to the clouds, orderly flying behind the leader, not noticing that on their backs they had uninvited passengers, our forest munchkins.

From the bird's-eye view, our travelers observed the panorama, but the forest and the city seemed like small specks, and the rivers and lakes were like bright ribbons and strips.

Our friends sat so comfortably on the soft backs of the birds that they did not leave their seats even at nights when the flock settled on trees to relax.

Episode 7

The Circus and the Ballgame

Our travelers flew over forests, deserts and lakes on the backs of the swallows. They met many dawns and dusks on their way and saw how the moon rose and disappeared.

Once when the swallows were choosing a grove to rest the night quite near some small town, our elves decided to go there to see what was going on. They agreed in advance, however, that in the morning they would return to their companions, the swallows.

The first one to visit the town was Draggle Tail Sorcerer, who soon came back running to his frolicking fellows with pleasant news.

"Come on, follow me!" he shouted. "I found something wonderful!"

The elves rushed after him, finding fabric tents pitched over a large area, and began to look into all the cracks and holes. The braver ones climbed the ropes to the roofs of the tents, hoping that the inside view would be better there.

Then came Murzilka in his narrow boots with long socks, barely keeping up with his brothers. All out of breath, Murzilka asked:

"What is it, gentlemen, what is it?"

"A circus, a real circus!" said Dr. Ointment, looking into the slit.

"Circus? Is there a circus?!" cried aloud Murzilka. "Let me in now, I love the circus!"

Although they could not clearly see through the gaps, the pixies did not move from the tent and closely followed all the exercises in the circus, clapping from time to time with their little palms.

"Gentlemen," suggested suddenly Topsy-Turvy with arms akimbo, "shouldn't we give a special circus performance? We've not found such fun for a long time."

"Excellent idea! Wonderful! That's Perfect!" rang from all directions.

The sprites settled nearby in anticipation of the night and the moment when the owner of the wandering circus would go to sleep.

As soon as the door was closed behind him, the elves crept through the cracks and openings into the tent.

So started a mess and merriment beyond imagination. Dr. Ointment was the first to jump on a horse. He was followed by a little man named Vault, who leaped like a clown through the paper hoops held by Hairlip and Father Beardie, Together with Dr. Ointment, they rode the horse with loud applause from everyone in the circus. Ten acrobats tiptoed on a tightrope, and the poles often toppled on the heads of the audience, which included the rest of the elves. That, however, did not prevent the little people from cheering the artists.

A not very successful performance happened with a rolling ball: The acrobats with whizzers on their heads flew off, and the ball passed over them, but they escaped and were scared a little without causing themselves any harm.

Feather Headed Murzilka perched on a podium for the whole performance playing the circus director, shouting and ordering.

No one, however, listened to him, no matter how angry he acted.

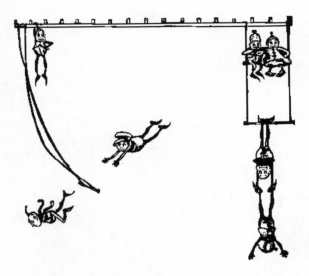

By the morning, the audience and the tiny artists and acrobats left the circus. Their hands were sore from applauding, and Murzilka was quite hoarse from shouting. Everybody was happy with their pranks and eager to find a new entertainment.

The poor circus owner could not understand what had happened during the night at the circus: Things were in disarray, paper wraps were on the floor, benches were scattered apart, and the horse was tired. While he brought everything back in order, the elves returned to their resting places on the swallows and went off again with them at first sunlight.

The elves loved their circus performance so much that they looked forward to a chance to land and have a new adventure.

Draggle Tail Sorcerer managed to learn from the conversation of two swallows that the whole company was going to relax in the nearest area for the whole day soon.

Indeed, shortly the swallows camped in the forest near a big city and settled in the trees to rest.

The elves climbed down to the ground near a field on a nearby meadow, where a large team played some game. On the ground was marked a quadrangle, and a man with a long stick stood in each corner, while in the middle was one with a ball. The player threw the ball to one of the four in the corners. The latter cast the ball with the stick to the next one, while two others had to run around the quadrangle. Several people standing near the rectangle threw the ball back when it flew over the line.

Judging by the excitement of the players and their fans, the game was fine and fun, and the brownies decided to play it the same way. But where could they get the sticks and balls?

Draggle Tail Sorcerer went to find them and returned with a beaming face.

"I found, really found them!" he shouted, waving his cap. "Follow me, it's not far from here."

Indeed, a few steps away was a store of gymnastic stuff.

The elves climbed through the open windows inside. Soon, their cheers announced their discovery.

Armed with sticks, balls and wire mesh for the faces, they quickly jumped down and hurried to the place of the game. Murzilka took only an iron wire mask. He was afraid that he would get hurt and decided that the mask could protect him.

Those who did not play sat on the fence and benches, and the others took up their sticks and began the game.

Harelip, forgetting his old age, ran as a good hare within the defined area, ahead of the flying ball all the time. Father Beardie together with Dundunduk played on the sidelines, arousing the admiration of others, while Dr. Ointment puffed and blew running with a stick on his shoulders from one place to another.

Murzilka was wearing the face mask, standing aside and watching the play. He made some comments from time to time.

The game continued until the evening, and it became quite dark before the pixies carried the sticks and balls back to the warehouse. It was a clear night with a myriad of southern stars and a gentle, bluish light of the moon.

The elves came over the fence and ran in their sponge boots to the place where the swallows rested, quietly waiting for the morning for departure.

After many adventures, the swallows, half-dead from fatigue, had flown almost half around the world. They landed with our invisible brownies on the shores of Italy.

The elves, who had not become tired of the journey at all, ran in hurry to get acquainted with this new foreign country.

Book 3
Welcome to Europe

Episode 8

Singing Lessons and William Tell

In Italy, the elves found orange and lemon groves, pomegranates and myrtles, grapes and roses growing everywhere. A far-off fire-topped mountain, shrouded in a pinkish-purple veil of fog, could be seen in the distance.

"I do love it here! What a beautiful place!" constantly cried Murzilka.

Running about in their sponge boots, the forest folk noticed a small, beautiful building nearby, a sonorous singing drifting from the windows.

"What admirable people are these Italians," said Dr. Ointment, "wherever you go, you can hear singing."

"Gentlemen," replied Draggle Tail Sorcerer, "let's take a look at who is singing."

"Let's see!" said every elf together. Murzilka was the first and fastest to jump on a partition standing at the window and begin to look inside. Pinwheel and Draggle Tail Sorcerer followed him in a hurry as well as the riders Skipjack, Popeyed and others. Topsy-Turvy climbed on the almond tree growing next to the window, on the very top of which sat Dundunduk and all others.

"Here they learn to sing!" said Dr. Ointment to everybody.

"They even teach a chorus," confirmed Doono and Dunno, sitting on the ball at the window.

"Hush, gentlemen, be quiet!" shouted Murzilka, "you are disturbing my listening."

Doono with Dunno, meanwhile, climbed through the window crack into the room. As soon as the students finished the class and the guard locked the door, they opened the windows, and the whole gang burst into the classroom. Putting four elves on guard, the rest took their places on the bench.

"Who will be our conductor?" asked Popeyed.

"Gentlemen, make me the conductor, please!" shouted back Murzilka.

"Come on, you as the conductor?!" laughed Dr. Ointment. "No, gentlemen, let's ask Harelip to be our conductor! He knows more about music than anyone else here."

"Right, right!" agreed everybody.

Harelip climbed on the chair, reached for the baton, and began to conduct.

The elves were master singers, so the hall soon sounded with choral songs. Dundunduk, Father Beardie and Dr. Ointment, who turned out to have a deep bass voice, showed great zeal.

First the little people sang one song, then another. Finally they pulled out of the lecterns some notes left in the room and were trying to memorize an unknown piece when the guards shouted, "The teacher is coming!"

The menacing baton of the conductor and the sheets of music were thrown on the floor, and our pranksters found themselves in the yard in no time.

"Who has made this mess in the classroom?" the teacher asked the school guard.

"Ha! Ha! Ha! This is us!" answered all the elves, but the professor could not hear their voices, tiny and distant as the buzzing of flies.

The forest brownies would definitely have stayed a while in Italy, but the swallows did not like to linger long in one place. One day soon, they gathered together again and hit the road. Soon our imps, soaring with the swallows, saw the mountains of Switzerland ahead.

On their way they passed high, snowy peaks and peered down on both a bottomless abyss and frantic waterfalls. On the slopes they saw verdant forests, and pastures stretched on unreachable heights where alpine goats and chamois were grazing. Picturesque valleys and lakes perched at the foot of the huge mountains, and great eagles hovered in the clouds.

The elves, however, paid little attention to all this and waited impatiently for the swallows finally to go back down to earth.

Finally, their desire was fulfilled, and the tired swallows, choosing a convenient place, decided to stop for a rest.

Once they got to the top of the mountain, Draggle Tail Sorcerer landed first on the field and immediately shouted to his comrades:

"Oh, look, here are a target and arrows!"

"Should we take them and try them somewhere in a secluded spot?" proposed Murzilka.

No sooner said than done! Tiny hands seized their discoveries and with great difficulty started up the hill; the porters were soon climbing with sweat pouring down. Only Murzilka did not carry anything, running and fussing more than the others as usual.

Finally, they got to a shady glade in the dense forest and put up the targets.

Each of our elves shot arrows in turn, but only Popeyed hit the spot.

"Bravo, bravissimo, Popeyed!" shouted his brothers, "you are an excellent shooter!"

"Bah!" grumbled the offended Murzilka, "He is an excellent shooter? I'd like to see him compete with me."

"Come then and shoot," his fellows said.

"Not me, I'm not going to spoil my hands," said Murzilka arrogantly.

"Hey, enough, don't be sulky! Listen better to what I'll tell you," Dr. Ointment said.

The crowd threw down the bow and arrows and surrounded the narrator.

"A few hundred years ago in Switzerland lived a man named William Tell. He was known throughout the country as the most accurate and skillful shooter of them all, and that meant something in a country where almost every resident shoots better than Popeyed...."

The beginning of the story about William Tell was so interesting that our forest people were all ears.

"The neighbors loved their brave and accurate shooter Wilhelm," said Dr. Ointment, "except the evil chief of the village, who constantly harassed him. One day the chief got so cruel that he called William Tell and said to him,

"Listen, people say you're the best shooter around. Prove it indeed: Shoot an apple which will be sitting on the head of your son!"

The terrified father trembled. "Have mercy! Let's not tempt fate to find misfortune!" he cried, "My hand may shake, and then I'd shoot the head of my child. You can do with me whatever you want, but please, release me from this fear."

But the chief did not listen to the laments of the father and did not take back the words spoken.

"Father, what are you afraid of?" asked the little son of Tell. "Would such a shooter as you are ever have a miss? Enough! I'm not afraid, so bring an apple here. Shoot, dear Father, and don't be afraid!" exclaimed the brave child, looking around proudly. The brave boy set the apple on his own head.

A shot rang out, and the eyes of the audience saw the shocked and shaken father and the smiling face of the son with the plowed apple on his head."

"What's a boy!" blurted out all the elves. "True grit! It's scary even to think about such things!"

"Why is that scary?" said the boastful voice of Murzilka behind a tree. "If you want, I'm ready to do the same."

"Don't brag, Murzilka," said Dr. Ointment. "Cut it out, silly!"

"No way, I'm not afraid!" shouted Murzilka. "I am not! Bring an apple—."

Several busy brownies went off to the nearest gardens for apples. They found a few very large apples, several times larger than the head of Murzilka, so it was easy to get them. With difficulty they dragged back their heavy burden.

"Really, do you really want to shoot these apples?" wept our little coward, now frightened till death. He did not know that the brothers would take his boasting seriously.

When they put an apple on his head, he trembled and cried with an anxious voice, "Popeyed, shoot first the apple lying on the ground; if you hit it in half, then I'll let you to do that, otherwise—never!"

Popeyed aimed, and in a second the apple split in halves.

"Oh, unlucky me," sobbed Murzilka, "Popeyed, darling, aim higher! If you shoot me in the head, then what will happen?"

"Don't worry, I shall not split you! Stand still!"

The brownie braggart was shaking all over, but his brothers, knowing that he was absolutely safe, wanted to wean him from boasting once and forever.

The elves surrounded poor Murzilka. Doono and Popeyed bent the bow. An arrow whistled, but at the same time, there was a desperate cry, never ever heard before by the pixies in their life.

Everyone rushed to Murzilka. He was very much alive and lay on the ground, shaking like someone in fever.

"Oh, you killed me, murdered Murzilka!" he groaned. "Oh, don't come! I am dead, you shot my little head."

A long, friendly laughter rang out over the quivering elf. He gently lifted up his head and noticed the good-natured laughter of his brothers. That left him really angry.

Episode 9
German School and France

"Gentlemen," said Draggle Tail Sorcerer loudly the next morning, "I just found out today that our swallows are ready to go!"

"Where are they going?" wondered the brownies. "What country?"

"They did not name the country," said Draggle Tail Sorcerer, "but they said that it will be the state where Germans live."

"That country is called Germany" said Dr. Ointment.

"Wonderful! Then, we shall see this Germany," shouted Popeyed. "I am very interested in this land. Hurry, my friends, let's go to the swallows, so they will not leave without us."

Everybody followed this advice and ran to the resting place of the swallows. An hour later, the elves were perched on their places on the pilgrim birds and flying towards the new country.

The swallows were in the air a great while before they came to Germany. Cities, forests, rivers, mountains flashed before the eyes of the elves until finally their birds landed in a small German town. They landed on a roof with a sign that said "Schule."

"What does this sign mean?" asked Murzilka. "Though I know German well, I've never heard such a word."

"Your German is pretty poor if you do not know that 'Schule' means a school," said Dr. Ointment.

"I mean, I knew, but I forgot....," mumbled Murzilka. "But if it is a school, let's check what they are teaching there."

The little people looked in the window. They saw that the students were packing their books and preparing to leave. Our pranksters waited until the pupils came out, and then the whole crowd moved into the classroom.

The first thing that drew their attention in the school was a huge ball, standing on high legs.

"What is it? What is this ball?" raised voices from everywhere.

"This ball is called the globe," explained Doono. "It shows the seas, land, mountains, rivers, and cities."

"What a thing," said our surprised elves. "Is the Earth round?"

"Of course, it is round," said Doono. "Do you want me to show you on this globe the places we have visited together with the swallows?"

"Yes, please, show us!" shouted all.

Doono jumped up on the bench in one nimble leap. Still, no matter how high the bench, Doono could reach the globe only with difficulty, so to get a little higher, he stacked some books to stand on.

"Listen," he said when he was perched upon his pile, "let's start."

Doono solemnly began to point out places on the globe, showing China, India, Egypt, Italy, Switzerland and Germany. Dr. Ointment, Popeyed and Skipjack climbed on his bench and threw out their hands in surprise. Dunno also tried to climb up there, but he could not.

Doono was about to find Russia when Murzilka ran into the classroom.

"Forget about the globe, let's go!" he cried. "Follow me. There is another classroom, more interesting with a pulpit and benches."

The elves rushed into the other room and immediately settled on the benches, pulled down the books from the desks and began to read aloud.

Those who did not get a place on the benches sat down on the floor without hesitation.

Several elves sat at the teacher's chair Incidentally, Dr. Ointment took a long cane and constantly corrected misbehaved pupils.

Murzilka also climbed on the pulpit, and, you would not imagine what he did! He jumped on the shoulders of the doctor! For such a lack of respect for his teacher, the elves took him on a high chair and put a paper stocking hat on his head. The elves roared with laughter, looking at Murzilka.

The lesson lasted for a long time and ended only in the late evening, when the tower bells tolled 8 p.m. Our elves threw down their books and rushed through the open window to their swallows.

But alas! The swallows had not waited for the woodland sprites this time, but went without them.

After the departure of the swallows, our forest brownies began to think that they had nothing left to do in this distant land and almost decided to go home by foot.

Murzilka, however, did not want to go back yet.

"We are so close to France!" he cried. "How can we miss this wonderful country which sets a tone for the fashion trends around the whole world? I'd love to go there and see how dandies dress now—my suit is very worn out. Please, before we return home, let's go to France. It is such an interesting country."

Murzilka kept talking for a long time. At first, the little forest people did not want to hear about it, but, finally they gave way to his requests and agreed to visit France so that they could just go home from there.

The elves rested, put on their sponge boots, and took the road.

Traveling from town to town, they came to a seaside resort at last, which was famous for its medicinal baths.

It was a delightful town, full of flowers, which attracted a lot of people every year.

Our pixies were just in time for the bathing season and, of course, did not want to lag behind the others. Murzilka was the first who learned that everybody bathed in suits. It would not be a bad thing, he thought, to get some bathing outfits—but where to get them?

The whole day our elves ran across the city until finally they found a warehouse of toys.

Hundreds of tiny hands began to rummage through the drawers and—oh joy!—among other stuff, they pulled out puppet costumes. Although these did not fit the sprites well, if tied up and tucked around in some ways, it was possible to put them on.

The pixies dressed in the ballroom muslin skirts instead of jackets and in hats of various styles instead of bathing bonnets. At the end, it turned into a funny masquerade, and the elves themselves could not look at each other without laughter.

They ran quickly through the streets and approached the shore. The sea—calm, majestic, and smooth as glass—lay before them; water waves lulled the beach and flooded the sand.

The imps jumped into the cool water like bouncing balls, sporting and playing in it as they stayed on the land because they could not drown in the sponge boots even if they dove to the bottom.

Laughter, noise and shouts were heard in the evening air, but only by the fish and the waves.

"Ah, the sea blew away my dress! My shorts! My shoes!" rang constantly their cheerful voices.

"And my wonderful hat, my top hat!" yelled Murzilka, who did not dare to leave his tall hat even when bathing.

After scampering about for a while in the water, the elves went to a grove, where they spent the night among the fragrant flowers.

Early in the morning, the elves woke up and, as usual, went wandering around the city. Soon the railway station attracted their attention.

The passengers were in a hurry to take their seats in the cars, as the train was to start in a few minutes.

The elves without waiting climbed on the roofs of the cars and considered themselves comfortable there. Soon came the third call, and the train departed at full speed, taking with it our tiny travellers.

Fields and forests flashed in front of them as a filmstrip. They stopped at stations shortly, and the train raced further and further.

One night the elves noticed a huge city with high buildings and monuments in the misty distance. Doono hastened to inform his brothers that they were close to Paris, the main city of France.

Soon the train actually stopped, and the elves, jumping to the ground, found themselves so crowded among the hustle and bustle so that they could hardly get out of it.

Despite the late hour, the streets were teeming with people, and the myriads of street and window lights turned the night into day.

The sprites, carried away by the crowd, moved along the boulevards, where a countless mass of the people walked.

Suddenly they missed Murzilka. Nobody had even noticed when he disappeared. In great concern the elves stood in front of a brightly lit store, not knowing what to do.

Suddenly a familiar voice rose, and their troublesome hero jumped out of the doors of the store, packed with fashionable fabrics.

"This is for a suit, this one for a vest, and this is for a coat" he explained, pointing to small sample pieces that the clerks apparently threw away on the floor.

After spending the night in a garden, the elves began sightseeing again at dawn, but the city looked much worse in the daylight than in the nightlights. Even the river Seine, on which Paris stands, seemed not particularly broad and beautiful.

Finally, our elves found themselves growing worn out and weary.

Episode 10
The Bicycles and Lawn Tennis

"News, dear gentlemen, news!" Draggle Tail Sorcerer exclaimed to wake up the elves. "I've just learned something very interesting!"

He woke before the others and went to a street right where people were hanging posters. On those posters in large letters was printed: "Bike racing competition to be held this morning in the country."

"This is a must see!" the Sorcerer cried. "Get up now, we don't have much time!"

In a second, the brownies were ready; even Murzilka kept up with the others.

Quickly they went to the announced location where the race was to be held and climbed a hill where they could see all the events.

Soon at a signal, more than 20 bikes with riders roared off in competition.

"Gee whiz," said Dr. Ointment, observing the cyclists closely. "They're moving without horses and without steam, and really quickly—like birds."

"I wish we had a bike for travel," said Pinwheel to Doono.

"Of course, not a bad idea," said Doono, bouncing.

"Listen, it just came to my mind," suddenly said Draggle Tail Sorcerer. "When these cyclists end their run and go to rest, we will pick a pair of bikes and pedal home on them."

"Yay! This is ingenious!" cried the elves together.

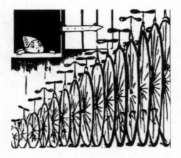

"I'll be ahead of everyone," bragged Murzilka, "and therefore I ask for my own bike."

"That would be wonderful," said Dr. Ointment, "but I am worried that after this run many bikes may be broken."

"That will not be a worry!" said Draggle Tail Sorcerer in response. "There is a workshop nearby, so we'll fix everything."

So they did. After the race was over and everybody had gone to rest, leaving the bikes in the workshop, the elves hurried there and immediately went to work repairing the bikes. The hammers clattered, the benches bustled, and the work was humming. By morning all the bikes were ready.

"But how do we fit on the bikes?" asked Doono when everything was ready.

Indeed, the bikes were too small to carry our crew of elves. Murzilka suggested that five of our brownies should sit with each other on the backs, but his proposal was not approved.

The pixies paused and pondered until finally Harelip invented a reasonable solution, which created enough room for everyone.

He managed to make a stick fit through the seats of three bikes in a row. On each such stick sat 15 elves; others clung to the handle, wheels and backs of the bikes. With singing and great racket rode the elves on their cleverly crafted "train."

Our little woodland people made the bicycles run quickly, and soon the city disappeared. The travelers found themselves on good highways where the riding got even faster.

The elves stopped on the road very rarely and only to relax, have lunch or breakfast, and then they wheeled on and on until one day they arrived at the English Channel that separates France from England.

"Yay! Yay!" shouted Pinwheel. We have reached the border of France."

"Yay!" echoed hundreds of voices.

"Brothers! England is now at our doorstep. Let's go to England! After all, it is worth a look, this country!" suggested Dr. Ointment.

"It's actually worth it! Let's do that!" they all agreed, jumping off the bicycles.

"Bah! How can we go to England if we don't have a horse?" Murzilka sighed.

"We have sponge boots," answered Father Beardie, the first to put on the waterproof shoes.

His example was followed by others, and soon the whole crowd walked together on the water surface. One, two, three—and the elves were already on the opposite bank.

"Here is the city! An English town!" shouted Doono.

The sprites did not like much the first English city, so they went on. Everywhere on the way they found factories and coal mines. Skipjack offered to go down into a coal mine, but Murzilka was dashed with terror.

"What? Do you want me to soil my French pants? No, never!" he cried.

"Why should you spoil them?" asked Skipjack.

"Do you think I'll walk on my head in your mines and the coal will not stick to me?" snapped Murzilka. "Besides, it is very dangerous to drop down into the mine."

"You are a coward," laughed Skipjack.

"I'm not afraid for myself, but for you," replied Murzilka in an offended tone.

The descent into the mine did not take place.

A few days later, the elves came to a beautiful garden, situated in an extensive and fragrant park, where they decided to relax and live.

Half of the travelers were looking for flowers to make a home. The other half, consisting of more curious elves, made themselves invisible and ran into the house to find out about the owner.

Half an hour later, they came back and reported the news they had learned. The owner was a rich Englishman, and he had a lot of rarities.

"What rare guns and swords he has hanging in the office!" admired Popeyed, talking to Harelip and Bear.

"What a library he owns!" said Father Beardie to Reader, a great lover of books.

"Brothers, our host is a doctor!" said Doono.

Dr. Ointment whopped for joy when he learned that the owner of the cottage also was a doctor.

"That's lovely! That's nice!" he said, pacing back and forth. "I can go with him to the patients, I can help him to write recipes .... Perhaps, we even can arrange a consultation together for a patient."

"Hm, I do not care whether or not our host is a doctor," said Pinwheel. "I am only glad that he has a lot of pears, grapes and plums. I hope that he will not refuse to treat us."

"I do not think he will do that," decided Quik. "Englishmen are stingy people."

"They are not stingy!" intervened Dundunduk, who stood nearby.

"No, they are avaricious. You just do not know."

"No, they are not stingy!"

No one knew how the dispute would have ended if suddenly Murzilka had not shown up.

He ran out of breath, and when he appeared to his fellows, could not utter a single word for a long time.

"Tell us, what happened? What did you see?" asked the elves, surrounding him from all sides.

"Oh, I've seen ... what I've seen! If you knew what I saw!" said finally Murzilka.

"Well, well, what?"

"Give a sigh, then I'll say ..."

"Here you go!" growled Skipjack. "Does he ever say anything worthwhile? He only knows about his suits."

"Wrong guess! I do not quite want to talk about my suits, by the way!" said Murzilka importantly.

"So tell us as soon as possible!" cried the elves in unison.

"Just a minute. I need to catch my breath. Well, now I can begin. Listen and do not interfere ...."

"I was walking through the park looking for a spot to relax. Suddenly I saw a huge meadow. Uh, I thought, what could it be? I pondered a lot, but could not guess. However, I hid behind a bush and waited."

"A few minutes later, several ladies and gentlemen came, placed some mesh and steel structures with the help of spatulas, and began to throw a small ball."

"Ladies and gentlemen," said one of the men, "whoever would like to play lawn tennis, come here."

"Yeah," I thought, "then this game is called lawn tennis." Meanwhile, those gentlemen ran to play after the call. They were all dressed in wonderful costumes, probably sewn on purpose for this game. Even their shoes were made for the suits."

"They should still be there in a clearing, so let's run there now," Quick broke Murzilka's story.

"Wait, let me finish the story well!"

But the little people, as you can see, got tired of Murzilka's long story and ran after Quick to find themselves on the spacious field, where a large company just was ending their game of lawn tennis.

The pixies closely followed the play, and as soon as the people went away, leaving all the equipment on the ground, Quick offered to play a game of lawn tennis like humans. "What do you think, shouldn't we try the game?"

"Let's play, of course, let's play!" agreed the elves. Immediately they began to transfer the mesh net, blades, balls and other accessories for the game to the other end of the clearing, where they thought it would be much easier for them to play.

"Oh, no, I cannot play yet. Wait until I craft a costume for the game," begged Murzilka.

"Bah! Sew, if you like, but we'll play!" they answered him.

Offended, Murzilka left and did not show up for a long time. He pulled out of his pocket a carefully folded package which contained his collection of fabrics from Paris. Then he chose the brightest one and began to cut a suit, hat and two pairs of tiny shoes. With the help of two other elves, Needle and Thread, he made himself a full suit for the game.

"How good I am!" he said, putting on his new outfit.

While Murzilka sat and sewed, on the lawn under the chestnut trees arose a racket, roar and fun. The elves were amused with the new game and laughed themselves to tears over their comical adventures.

Doono hit Harelip with the ball, who could not stand and fell, dragging Dunno behind him, who in turn pushed Pinwheel. Reader got stuck under the net and cried in his shrill voice over the whole meadow. Under another net lay Draggle Tail Sorcerer, and Bully stretched before him.

"Here I am!" a squeaky Murzilka's voice rang among general merriment.

The brothers all turned, and a friendly laughter greeted the gaudy elf.

"Ho-ho-ho! Ha-ha-ha! Hee-hee-hee," the elves shook with laughter, looking at the strange costume of Murzilka. "Here is a scarecrow! Hee-hee-hee ...."

"You are the scarecrows!" angrily answered the dandy. "I'll not bother even to talk to you, ugly ducklings!"

Murzilka turned to leave, but his brothers get him back, promising never to laugh at him again.

Dr. Ointment even hung his hat and cane on a stick so they would not be wrinkled.

"Skipjack, dear! Come to me! I really want to play with you! You're just as clever as I am," meantime commanded Murzilka.

Episode 11

Skating in London and the Mill in Holland

One week went by, then another, while the forest folk still lived in the villa of the English doctor.

"What about wandering to another place, dear gentlemen?" said Quick. "Though it is great here, we are getting bored, finally, with sitting at the same place."

"That's right!" replied the elves. "Where could we go?"

"Oh, of course, to the capital, to London!" answered Murzilka. "I want to see how the English mods dress."

"Point taken. To the capital!" said Harelip.

In the evening, when the heat of the day declined, the pixies put on their boots, slid down their hospitable rooftop, and set off quickly to the capital.

All night they walked through forests and fields, and in the morning, with the first sunbeams, the fair city with towers and churches appeared.

"Fellows, let's rest a little here!" proposed Draggle Tale Sorcerer. "By the way, Dr. Ointment, please, tell us something about this city. You are the scientist and know everything."

"I know lots about London," said Murzilka. "Do you want me to tell you the tale? Even my checkered coat that you all are laughing about, was sewn in the latest London fashion."

"Enough talk!" said Pinwheel. "We'd better go before it gets dark in the city."

Clouds of smoke and dust from factory chimneys covered the city. Machinery, trams, and omnibuses flew in all directions. The elves were confused by such a fuss and bustle.

"No, I do not like it here!" Murzilka muttered, holding his tall hat with both hands.

"You were dying to come here! Oh, Murzilka, Murzilka, the feather head!" his brothers mocked him.

Looking around a bit and getting used to the noise of the streets of London, the elves gradually began to feel comfortable in Great Britain.

They rode on railway cars, which raced with extraordinary speed from one end of the city to another. They wandered their way to the ships and steamers floating on the River Thames (where the city of London stands). Most of all, though, they were thrilled with the three-story bridges over the River Thames. Under the bridges, ships flew; across the bridges, trains and trams rumbled; and on them, omnibuses and pedestrians hurried.

"Heigh, what a city!" the brownies admitted after such sightseeing.

A week in London flew by in an instant. On Sunday morning, the elves woke early and went out to the street (they slept on myrtle branches in a rich garden).

The streets were remarkably quiet and calm: neither drivers nor pedestrians rushed by, the smoke did not pour from the factories, the shops were closed, and the city seemed empty.

"What could it be?" wondered the elves.

"Oh yes! I forgot to warn you," said Reader. "On Sundays, the British do not work and do not walk, but only go to church or stay at home and read the scriptures."

"What are we gonna do today?" Murzilka sighed.

"I know! Let's skate!" Skipjack said.

"What are you talking about? How can we skate in the middle of summer?"

"Are there skating rinks?" the elves asked.

"Let's go, follow me, I'll show you," Skipjack responded.

The crowd rushed behind Skipjack, who led them to a large round building with closed doors.

Harelip opened the door with one deft move, and a huge hall with a brilliant stone floor, smooth as glass, appeared before their eyes.

"Yay! How nice it is here. That's an artificial ice rink!" all cried.

"What is it? Look, I have more in store here!" Skipjack said laughing. "After all, special skates on wheels are needed to ride on the stone." Then, he showed a box of tiny skates to the astonished crowd.

"The ones with red wheels belong to me!" cried Murzilka, who had already noticed that painted pair of skates.

"Ok, they are yours. Skipjack laughed. "For who else? Only for you."

In an instant, all the elves put on the skates and started to frolic. The sprites had such great fun they had not enjoyed for a long time. Their faces reddened, their eyes shone, and jokes and laughter sounded everywhere.

The pixies played skating tricks of all kinds: They caught each other by their clothes and rolled in a long line on the rink, or they broke the chain and fell flying on each other, overthrowing onlookers to the delight of others.

Murzilka, of course, as usual, tried to convince the fellows that no one was a smoother skater than him.

"Look how nimble I am at riding on one leg," he said aloud to the rest of the brownies. "Look: one, two, three—."

Before he could finish saying "three," he stretched out on the floor.

"Ha, ha, ha! That is so clever!" the elves called.

"Nothing to laugh about," angrily answered Murzilka. "It was just an accident. That could happen to anyone."

He got up from the floor and limped over to the bench, apparently immediately losing his interest in skating on wheels.

Soon the elves had studied the city well, so they decided to go on to see new people and new cities.

"Brothers! Where shall we go now?" asked Harelip. "England is surrounded by water on all sides, so there is no overland way we can use. Do you want to go home over the Channel and France again or through another country, for example, through the Netherlands?

"Of course, through Holland! After all, we have already had a holiday in France," responded the imps.

"Well, let's hurry to it!" agreed Harelip, handing out the sponge boots to the elves.

Plunk, plunk, plunk ... tiny feet plashed through water.

"Hey, I see the bridge!" soon cried Popeyed.

"It's not a bridge, but a wooden fence to reduce water pressure," replied Dr. Ointment.

Then, he went on to explain that the Netherlands was formed from sand and silt, and the residents had to fight constantly with the sea so it would not flood the land.

Although the story of the doctor was very interesting, nobody listened because they all ran to the fence on the water and then through the walkways to the sand and the city seen in the distance.

Of course, they had some incidents on their way: The fence broke, and the elves almost fell into the water. But, in the end, they made it safely to the shore.

Suddenly the merry crowd stopped. They saw a roaring brook which drove strong mill wheels.

"How can we cross the creek?" asked Dr. Ointment.

"Let's swim across! Sail over! Hurry!" answered the brownies and rushed swimming.

"Dr. Ointment, give me a hand, and you Harelip, give me another!" shouted Doono.

"This way, by holding hands we can safely cross."

"Oh, brothers, help, I'm drowning! Help!" Murzilka shouted, choking.

"You won't go down! The water is not deep at all," said Dunno, laughing and swimming by him.

"How do you know? asked Feather Head.

"Stop it, don't fight!" intervened the others. "Here it is, and you can see the city."

Leaping ashore, the elves dried themselves and set off on the road.

Shortly after, the forest fellows found themselves in a large port city from where ships sailed to all the countries of the world. While some of them were coming back, others were leaving. The elves met black people from Africa during their walk, then Indians from India, and even a swallow friend with whom they had flown to Europe.

The brownies bustled around the city for a long time, listening to other languages and studying new people.

"I do not want to wander here any longer," said whimsical Murzilka, who soon got tired of everything. What's so interesting here? Let's get away to Amsterdam as soon as possible. There Peter the Great studied shipbuilding. I want to see the city. What can we do here?"

"Wait a minute!" said his brothers. "We'll see all the sights around here, then soon we'll go to Amsterdam."

Murzilka growled something sulkily and did not speak again until they left the city.

The next morning the elves washed with dew, sipped sweet nectar from the cups of tulip flowers at dawn and went their way onward.

By noon, they stopped to rest on the shady shore of a fast river.

"Gentlemen! A mill stands nearby. Should we go there?" asked Dr. Ointment.

"We'd love to!" said all the brownie brothers.

"Oh, I'll be a miller!" exclaimed Draggle Tail Sorcerer and tied a red checkered handkerchief on his head.

"Hey! Something is not right here!" cried the woodland people entering the yard. "It's the busy season, but the mill stands silent. Is the owner all right?"

"Brothers!" as if in answer shouted Draggle Tail Sorcerer. "I've just been in the house of the miller. Oh brothers, the poor man is dying. His wife and children are crying. People brought a lot of grain, but no one can grind it."

"Really?!" the elves interrupted him and took counsel on how they could help.

"How dare you take my red scarf? I wanted to make a Turkish bathrobe for myself!" suddenly broke in Murzilka, rushing to stand before Sorcerer.

"Ha, ha, ha," the others laughed. "Here's our Feather Head! When it's time to talk about how to help someone, he is concerned about that!"

"Shame on you!"

Confused, Murzilka quickly left, and the elves began to consider what would be a cure.

"Dr. Ointment, you're a great doctor! You know how to treat anything with herbs, so please, cure the miller. And you, Doono, please, go and find out whether this poor and his family need something," said the Harelip.

Dr. Ointment was pleased with his role and ran into the woods for herbs, and then he turned invisible and went into the house.

While the whole family was asleep, he mingled some medicine into the patient's drink, which should help him recover immediately.

Meantime, the forest folk fussed and bustled about the mill.

The work was in full swing in the hands of the elves, who decided to grind all the grain during a single night, so that the miller could go and sell the flour as soon as he felt better.

During the night, the miller stood up and drank the medicine prepared by the tiny doctor, not knowing what power was hidden in it.

In the morning, he woke up fresh and feeling as fine as if he never had been ill.

"O Lord, my God!" he wondered. "Last night I was so sick that I was expecting death, and today I feel completely happy and healthy. What a wonder—it's hard to believe!"

He put on his coat and went to the mill. He approached it with anguish because for more than four months, he was not there.

"The grain will be rotten and the mill must have collapsed. Before my illness, the entire roof was full of holes," he said to himself.

But what a surprise it was when the miller found the roof repaired, the mill wings fixed, and finely-ground flour packed in bags stored in rows.

Surprised, the miller stood in the midst of the mill with his mouth open.

"What godmother power is on our side!" the surprised man said, looking around with happy eyes on the kind deeds of our forest people. They were on the roof, and looking through the cracks, were glad about his happiness.

"Well, enough!" shouted Murzilka, falling from the roof. "That is nothing to look at! I ripped off my coat on this nasty roof. Let's go. Or I'll be completely without my long-tailed coat!"

"Do me a favor, stop complaining, Murzilka!" said Topsy-Turvy.

"Ah, ah, ah!" was suddenly heard.

Pinwheel, Quick and Bear had flown from the roof straight into the noisy stream.

"Well! I told you that we should leave, but no, you didn't listen, so have a bath now," said Murzilka happily, smiling at his soaking brothers.

"This disaster is not a disaster!" said Pinwheel, Quick and Bear, climbing out of the water. "Next time we will listen more carefully. As for the swimming, it really does not matter ...." They made it safely to the shore by stepping on a log.

"Murzilka, you started a quarrel again! What a mischief!" said Harelip to him. "We want to keep the board now, and you are still angry over trifles."

"What board?" asked Murzilka, easily passing from grumpy tone to a more friendly voice.

"How should we hurry home from Holland? Dr. Ointment advises us to travel south through Belgium, but Reader says that it is better to go north through Denmark, Norway and Sweden," said Harelip.

"Ahem, ahem!" Murzilka shook his head. "I also advise a trip through Belgium. There, they say, the best lace in the world is made. Maybe I'll find something for my costume, such as vintage frill."

"Ha, ha, ha!" was arose laughter among the elves. Murzilka was not angry that time, however, since he saw that his wish would be fulfilled.

Book 4
Long Journey Home

Episode 12

The Spindle, the Dentist, and the Laboratory

The sprites once more put on their sponge boots and invisible hats and set off. By evening, they came to Brussels, the main city of Belgium. There, as in Holland, they were amazed by the clean and tidy streets and the many gardens and flowers, especially tulips, decorating the houses with their washed windows sparkling in the sun. The Belgian women, as well as the Dutch, wore on their heads enormous bonnets with ribbons.

The elves ran to every corner of the city, climbing curiously into the houses and shops. Finally, they settled in a suburban garden for the night.

"Gentlemen," said Draggle Tail Sorcerer in a whisper. "I was looking through a crack in the fence and saw something amazing in the next yard. Perhaps we can take a look at what it is, couldn't we?

"You bet! Of course!" the elves answered.

It was a bright, moonlit evening. The wet grass was fragrant, and the quiet night sky flashed bright stars. Our brownies washed themselves with dew, and refreshed, climbed one by one over the fence to explore the Sorcerer's surprising discovery.

In the backyard, they found a broken spinning wheel, a spindle, and a flyer to keep the coils during winding.

"Ugh, what junk!" exclaimed Murzilka contemptuously.

"What's the worry? We'll fix the junk," said Father Beardie.

"Yeah, yeah! We'll fix and mend!" said the elves, jumping about with excitement.

"But it is inconvenient to work here," said Harelip. "It's better to move the stuff away where no one will get hurt."

Instead of answering, hundreds of tiny hands seized the broken items and dragged them with a great effort.

"Oh, seriously, it's above our strength!" Murzilka groaned, running back and forth, but not touching anything.

Suddenly a heavy wheel tilted on its side and, if the elves had not had their magic power, it would without doubt have killed many of them. All the imps rushed to help, and after much effort they finally managed to put everything in an unused corner of the park, near the river, where no one of the house residents ever came.

Until the morning, the little forest people worked over the wreckage. How happy they were when the broken and worthless objects turned to quite new ones, suitable for work, in their hands.

"What do we do now?" they asked each other.

"Oh, I have an idea!" Draggle Tail exclaimed. "I saw a lot of cotton nearby. You know, the kind which was growing in India in the fields. It's already washed and dried—quite ready for yarn. Shall we take it and spin it?

"Why do you need thread?" asked grumpy Murzilka.

"Why not? We'll spin the thread and weave a cotton fabric or make handkerchiefs. You never know what could be made of cotton!" answered Draggle Tail, rushing with several little pixies to the barn where the cotton was stored.

So, the work was humming for our elves!

Doono and Dunno spun the spindle, Dr. Ointment pulled the thread, Reader wound the yarn, Skipjack and Bear caught the balls, and others helped as much as they could, giggling about the buzzing spindle.

Murzilka, dressed in the latest fashion in a short coat, striped pants, and a newfangled tall hat with a lace handkerchief, ran and bustled among his brothers, pretending hard work.

When all the yarn was ready, the elves moved it into the barn, singing, and locked the door. Then they said goodbye to the floral cups which had sheltered them for the night, and set off, moving from one city to another until they came back to the border.

"Gentlemen," Harelip asked the others one morning, "Now we need to get to Austria. How do you want to do that? Shall we walk again or should we fly on birds?" "By walking, it's better to walk," answered the brownies in one voice.

"The trip is long," Harelip reminded them. We are in the south, and we need to go through Germany, where we already were, remember?"

"Yes, but then we did not see much in Germany," said Reader. "I'd really like to meet some scientists."

"We can stay there a little longer, especially because Murzilka would like to order a new suit in Berlin," said Harelip.

For many days the elves lived in Berlin, the capital of Germany. They were perfectly settled, especially Murzilka and Reader. The first elf swept all the shops, and the second one visited some German scientist every day, where he enjoyed reading old books.

Once Reader, Topsy-Turvy, Chinese Chi-ka-chi and Murzilka went together for a walk. When they passed one house, they heard heart-rending cries, which disturbed them.

"Oh, what is it?" our scared elves wondered, looking anxiously at the door.

Murzilka's knees failed him in horror.

"Uh! It's just a dentist who lives here," said Reader, who had slipped through the door and immediately come back. "He is pulling a tooth. Look at that!" he said to his brothers. "There are Dr. Ointment and Alchemist sitting on the window. Why are they there?"

Knowing that the brothers were there as well and there was no danger, our coward Murzilka stopped trembling and with his usual arrogance began to mock others.

"Why does this man yelling? How silly it is to shout! I am sure that he pretends, and it does not hurt at all," he said to Dr. Ointment, who was carefully observing the operation.

"I'd like to hear how you'd scream when your tooth is being pulled out!" said Dr. Ointment to Murzilka.

"You'd not hear a peep out of me, you'll see!" he replied.

"Well, let's see," the doctor said, winking to Alchemist, who was involved in drawing up different drugs.

Murzilka got pale as a white sheet, but still sat on the bench which the elves moved to him.

"Hold me, Alchemist, hold me tight, so I will not fall!" he said in a changed voice, his teeth chattering. "And you, Dr. Ointment, please, don't pull it immediately; you'd probably hurt me out of spite!" he cried to the doctor.

But as soon as Dr. Ointment appeared with the tongs, Murzilka stretched to his full height, shouted in an unnatural voice, quickly jumped to his feet, knocked Alchemist and the approaching doctor aside, and ran outside.

"What a coward!" said the brothers. "We were joking, and he almost came to be crazed with fear!"

That same evening, when the elves gathered together to share their impressions of the day, the Chinese told about Murzilka's adventure at the dentist.

"While you are laughing," Murzilka interrupted the narrator, not wishing everybody to know the story, "and while all of you are just wasting time running around, I discover something new every day doing serious science."

"Wow, what? You do science! Here we go, the inventor!" rang the mocking voices.

"Am I not?" Murzilka threw a glare at the doctor. "Here is a discovery. I went wandering around the city and came across a wonderful laboratory, which is an institution where all kinds of experiments take place with the use of special devices. Oh, if only you knew what I saw! Do you want me to take you there?"

"Oh, let's all go there!" Doono said.

"Yes, yes, let's go to the lab," picked up the rest of the flock.

The woodland people stood up from the grass and followed Murzilka, who was supposed to show the way.

He went ahead, walking haughtily and ceremoniously, until finally he stood in front of a large building and proudly pronounced, "It's here."

In a second, the forest brownies scattered into all corners of the rooms, staring at the mysterious tools and shells.

On one table was a microscope, a tool for examining the smallest objects by zooming to an enlarged view.

"Tah-dah, look!" shouted Bear in a weird voice, looking at a tiny insect in the microscope. Quick also took a glimpse and even squatted in astonishment. The insect seemed to him larger than a human.

In another corner, Father Beardie was grasping a green frog, which was watched by Tim through a magnifying glass.

The Chinese, who could draw really well, was glad to find different colors in the laboratory. He began to mix them while Doono pounded them into a powder in a mortar.

Dunno and Pinwheel began to warm up some liquid on an alcohol burner.

Nearby, Reader was fiddling with some retort (a glass vessel used for chemical experiments).

Seeing this, Father Beardie released the frog and ran to Reader without worrying about frightened frog, who jumped and leaped like crazy.

"Ahhh! Ah, help! Come here!" suddenly a shrill voice screamed.

The brothers looked at each other in fear and ran to the desperate cries.

What had happened? While the elves engaged in physical and chemical experiments, Murzilka went to an anatomical study room, where skeletons and the pictures of cut parts of the human body hung. At the sight of them, Murzilka got cold feet.

The elves also saw such pictures for the first time except for Dr. Ointment, who studied, of course, human anatomy, so Draggle Tail Sorcerer, who knew everything perfectly, began to teach the brothers.

"Look at this head, which is drawn on the blackboard," explained Draggle Tail. "It shows how many parts are in the head of a man—."

"And what is there in that dark room?" our little coward Murzilka suddenly interrupted him.

Dr. Ointment smiled and said nothing. He spotted at the front of this room a magic lantern and white screen where the pictures would project.

Without saying a word, he walked into the room, quietly inserted the magic lantern plate with a fly, a locust and a beetle painted on it, then turned on a tiny light bulb—and a white screen immediately zoomed the image of these insects by many times. It's hard to describe what horror fell fast on our merry crowd. The small audience embarked headlong out of the room.

The more mindful elves soon returned, though, and as soon as they knew what was going on, laughed to tears over their fear.

Gradually, all of them came back except poor Murzilka, who did not dare to enter the room, no matter what reassurance his brothers said.

Episode 13
The Zoo in Vienna

Having made a mighty mess and played enough, the elves went wearily to sleep in a garden. Before they slept, though, they packed all their belongings, as they planned to leave Berlin at dawn to continue the journey.

In the morning, our forest folk found the first train from Berlin to Vienna. Not too many travelers chose the early train, so the elves settled smiling in the first-class cars.

Murzilka made his place in front of the mirror that hung on the wall of the car. He wanted to admire himself all the way in spite of the fact that the other elves were laughing and joking about it.

Without a single incident arrived the sprites at the city of Vienna, capital of Austria, and they set straight off from the station to see the sights of the city.

Vienna is a beautiful city, and there of the brownies found lovely luxury homes, precious palaces and shining shops. The imps loved Vienna, especially Murzilka, who wandered with indescribable delight in all the things along the way.

"Oh, what stores, what houses, what luxury! Here everybody is even better dressed than in Paris!" he cried, stopping every minute.

His brothers, though, did not follow his fascination, for they were wide-eyed and wondering at the wolves, lions, and tigers painted on a large billboard at the corner of the street.

"Doctor," they all appealed to Dr. Ointment, "please, tell us what is said here on the poster."

The doctor explained that the poster was the announcement that on this day in the Zoological Gardens would be a wonderful show of wild animals from Africa. He offered to lead the brothers to the garden, and of course, they agreed.

When the elves reached the zoo, it was late at night when the visitors were gone, and the animals were all enjoying the evening in their enclosures.

Our brownies went at once into the first pavilion, where they saw all sorts of monkeys.

"Ha, ha, ha! What fantastic faces they make!" the pixies rocked with laughter, looking at the apes' grimaces.

"Hee, hee, hee!" laughed the monkeys in turn, looking at the elves.

After a good laugh with the monkeys, Father Beardie called out, "The turtles are nearby, and we'll want to take a look at them."

Father Beardie had not even finished his last words before our pixies surrounded him from all sides.

"Turtles," they all exclaimed. "Where is the way to the turtles? Take us to them now!"

The elves quickly ran to another room, with Murzilka, making a sour face, following them.

On the floor of the room a huge turtle rested.

"Dear Turtle, hello!" the elves cried, climbing onto her back.

"Hey, well, well! Faster! This way we'll not move from this place till the morning!" Popeyed drove the turtle with his arms akimbo.

"Wait, wait!" Murzilka cried, thinking that the turtle would run at a trot and that he might not keep up with the other forest folk. "Give me your hands, I too would like to ride on the turtle."

With a boost from the friendly brownies, Murzilka climbed on the back of the tortoise, but it did not get under way.

"Well, this is no fun," fussed Murzilka. "We'd better risking a ride on a lion or a tiger!"

"Why, Murzilka is talking sense!" answered the others, and the crowd ran racing to the beasts of prey.

As soon as they entered the pavilion which housed wild animals, there rose a terrible roar and cry from all corners. The beasts, which were sleeping peacefully in the corners of their homes before, rushed forward and began to raise a racket.

Murzilka, seeing that the animals were locked behind strong iron bars, tried to seem brave.

"I am absolutely not afraid of lions, tigers or panthers," he said.

"Well, dear Murzilka, don't you say that," said Sorcerer laughing. "We all know now how brave you are. Never mind talking about lions here—you are even afraid of mosquitoes and run away from them for a hundred miles."

The elves laughed, and Murzilka flushed with anger.

"I'm scared? Who, me? Oh, no, it's you, you are all cowards!" he cried. "Look, how I can tease this lion."

And having said that, Murzilka came to the cage and began to tease a lion with a stick, striking it on the bars of the cage.

The lion sullenly walked back and forth, first seeming to pay little attention to Murzilka, but suddenly he became angry and grabbed the iron bars of the cage with such force that the rods bent like reeds.

Hearing the roar of the lion, all the other animals began to bellow and lash out in their cages.

The tiger, with its mouth wide open, stuck his terrifying paw through the bars of the cage, eager to grab someone from the forest folk. The panther with bloodshot eyes began to beat its head against the cage, as if intending to break free.

The elves were terrified in earnest and got so confused that instead of getting out of the room, they rushed forward to the enraged animals.

The blame was on Murzilka. He was the first who started running and shouting to the brothers:

"Follow me, run! Here is the exit! Or the lions will gobble you!"

The elves ran behind Murzilka, pushing and crushing each other; passing by the elephants, monkeys, parrots, but not paying any attention to them. Some of the brownies jumped on an ostrich they met on their way and rode it through the garden to the gates. The elves calmed down only when they found themselves far from the zoo.

Episode 14

A Snowman in Warsaw
and Home, Sweet Home!

"Gentlemen!" said the Harelip, "what do you think about our departure? After all, it is already winter here. I believe we should hurry up, so the snowflakes will not see us, or they might perhaps bury us.

"Sure, let's go away!" answered all the elves together.

Harelip handed out the sponge boots to everybody, and the elves began to walk quickly and easily.

By noon of the fifth day, our busy brownies approached a big city.

"Wait!" warned Draggle Tale Sorcerer to his brothers. "I'll run ahead to find out what the city it is and come back soon."

"Go, go!" the brothers answered. "We'll rest a little while and find some forest flowers."

The imps drank floral juice, which they found in the late autumn flowers, rested in the colorful cups, and climbed on the trees, but still Draggle Tale did not come back.

The elves began to worry in earnest, about whether anything had happened to him when their sensitive ears caught the notes of Draggle Tale's cheerful song, and soon they saw the tiny singer.

"Why so late? You scared us!" the brothers reproached him.

"Wait, do not yell, I'll tell you everything, but just let me catch my breath," Draggle Tale said smiling.

"Well, well, well?" the elves hurried him.

"Oh, my brothers," began Draggle Tale, sitting on a tree stump, "we are close to home, to Russian—."

"What are you saying?" interrupted the elves.

"I say the truth, because this city in front of us is Warsaw!"

"Yay!" the elves were happy.

"What a beautiful city Warsaw is, if you only knew," continued Draggle Tale when everybody calmed down. "I checked everything there: what sort of bridges crossed the river Vistula, what palaces and churches are in the city and how many gardens they have."

"Why dally? Let's go there now!" asked
Harelip. In an instant the whole band was
on the road to the city seen in the distance.

During their talks and arguments, our
brownies did not notice how a dark
autumn night full of myriads of stars and
cold fresh air came on the earth.

In spite of the late hour, the city was busy.
Carriages and cars raced on the lighted
streets, while on the sidewalks pedestrians
rushed back and forth, admiring the
products displayed in the store windows.

The elves gaped and gathered in the crowd among the other pedestrians, giggling at every push. Only Murzilka worried a lot. He scanned the passers-by, jumped into a carriage, and finally entered the opened doors of the stores. All that he saw in Warsaw greatly pleased and enthralled him.

Who knows how long they would be having fun if suddenly the air had not flashed with white and fluffy snowflakes?

"Well, well!" sang the snowflakes, circling in the air. "We are flying from afar! We'll decorate and cover everything with snow!"

As soon as the elves heard these familiar voices, they ran away.

That was what they were afraid of: First, the snowflakes could easily snow them in; second, they were all dressed in light suits and could freeze.

The elves rushed through the streets for a long time, looking around helplessly for a place to shelter, but the big stone houses were barricaded against our brownies with closed windows which discouraged the pixies from staying in them.

Finally, the elves saw a big garden, enclosed with a high fence.

"There, there!" doctor called.

The brownies quickly set off after the doctor and went into the garden.

The garden gate was closed, but the elves deftly climbed through the cracks one after another, and soon all of them were in the garden. The snow covered the fields and alleys and crunched under tiny feet. The elves shivered in despair and did not know where to warm themselves when suddenly Murzilka shouted in a voice not his own.

"Look, gentlemen, look! I found a palace!"

"Palace?!" the elves shouted with surprise in one voice, and forgetting about the cold and fatigue, ran to Murzilka.

To their surprise, our brownies followed Murzilka to a warm pavilion in a corner of the garden where particularly delicate plants were kept during winter! There was indescribable joy when they opened the door with the help of the fern and settled to rest under the green leaves of roses and lilies, as if it were summer again, not late autumn with blizzard and snow!

It had been long since the elves slept so calmly and sweetly at night; green leaves swayed softly, lulling the little sprites, bending over them and quietly whispering to them sweet dreams about tropical countries where the palm trees grew and monkeys swung and colorful parrots sat on the branches of the wide tamarinds.

The brownies woke up late in a happy and cheerful mood.

"Oh, what a wonderful dream!" they said all together. "Aren't we in India again and sleeping in the Raja's garden?" asked Father Beardie and jumped on the window, from where he cried in joy, turning to his brother.

"Look how much snow is there! Come here now, everyone!"

The fact was that during the night a blanket of snow fell, which covered the lawn and walkway with a thick layer. The morning was cold, and the snow was not melting.

"Hee-hee-hee!" the elves giggled with delight. "Our native snow! How nice to see it again!"

"Gentlemen, let's make a snowman!" offered a little elf named Alchemist.

"Great idea!" agreed all the elves. "We will sculpt a snowman!"

"A giant snowman!" proposed Popeyed.

"Giant, yes, a giant!" the merry crowd shouted. "There is a lot of snow." The elves spilled out into the garden.

Their tiny feet sank into the deep snow, but the elves did not worry: They swept the whole garden and found a quite dark corner, where the greenhouse frames were installed during summer.

"Mmm, but how are we going make a giant?" asked Father Beardie. "We are so small."

"Well, what if," interrupted Murzilka in a hurry, "what if we'll make a 'life pyramid,' so one will be on the shoulders of another, and I will stand on the top and will supervise the work."

"You talk nonsense, as usual!" said Alchemist. "How can one work standing on each other as logs? We need to make a real pyramid structure."

"Of course, the real thing, like frames for the construction of houses," the woodland people agreed and began to collect dry twigs. An hour later, they had enough limbs to start the work.

Again, the elves made things hum in their small but busy hands! The pyramid construction grew taller and taller by the minute, and by noon it was ready.

"Enough!" said Harelip. "Now we'll bring the snow!"

"Snow, snow, snow!" cried the elves, and like ants, they hurried and hustled around the garden.

They began to build the foundation of the future giant, and all except Murzilka worked with enthusiasm. Pinwheel and Reader found eight red large carrots somewhere, which they brought with a scream of joy to the construction site.

"Oh, these will make beautiful hair and a mustache!" said the brothers and thanked Pinwheel and Reader for their discovery.

Father Beardie dragged huge lumps of snow, and Tim and Bear managed to make such big snowballs that the sprites just gasped in surprise. The work was in full swing, the snow was passed with lightning speed from the bottom up, and the foundation increased with each second. Of course, some incidents happened.

As soon as Pinwheel and Reader climbed to the top, our careless Reader fell from the scaffolds and flew headlong into the soft snow, from which his brothers pulled him with difficulty.

Their fear for him had just passed when Tim and Bear quarreled about something. In the heat of the argument, they dropped a lump of snow, which flew down until a desperate cry was heard from Murzilka; then came silence.

The horrified elves hurried to the spot and began hastily casting aside the snow under which Murzilka was buried.

"Oh-ho-ho!" Murzilka moaned in misery. "You killed Murzilka, killed this clever boy for no reason, no reason at all!"

"Well, we're sorry, but do not worry, Murzilka, and please forgive us. We did not mean to," said the confused Tim and Bear.

"Forgive you?" Murzilka pounced on them. "My tall hat was crushed, my suit was ruined, my new shoes got wet, and I should forgive you?"

"Come on, Murzilka!" Popeyed, Dr. Ointment and others tried to reason with him, but our dandy went on and on complaining and did not want to listen.

"I'll not forgive, no!" he shouted, waving his flushed fists. "I'll never forgive, and I do not want to work, I'll just sit here and will mingle so you'll know what it means to offend Murzilka next time.

Realizing that nothing could help, the brothers left him alone and began to work again.

Our elves had a lot of fun, uniting to complete the task; their laughter and hubbub rang over the garden.

Murzilka was angry and grumpy, but the gaiety of the others affected him as well. Soon he began to run back and forth in his usual manner, fussing around, giving advice and disturbing our busy brownies. He certainly did not do anything, but just shouted at the others. The elves did not pay attention to him and just smiled indulgently at his remarks.

"Gentlemen, we approach the head! Tell us, whom we will now sculpt?" wondered the top workers.

"Ah, it should be a Frenchman! Please, a Frenchman!" pleaded Murzilka.

"The French is the French," the elves agreed and set about finishing the head. When it was ready, Skipjack and the Chinese brought two large coal stones and inserted them for the eyes. They also painted a mouth, a nose and the ears. The carrots decorated the snowman's head as a mustache, a beard and four spiking hairs. In the right hand of the giant, Alchemist inserted the eighth carrot, so that it seemed as if the Frenchman pointed to something in the distance.

Finally, when everything was done, our little people hurriedly began to reassemble the pyramid structure.

Loud cheering joy burst out from a hundred voices when in front of the admiring crowd appeared the slender giant, lit by pink light of the setting sun.

The snowman came out really great, and not without reason the elves were in awe of their own work.

"Hooray, hooray!" thundered in the air.

In the sky, meanwhile, the stars lit up and blinked one after another. The elves moved into the warm pavilion, where they settled down for the night.

In the morning, the sun rose and peered into the corner of the garden where the snowman stood. Indeed, the sun smiled to see the creation of our little people, but because of that smile, all the snow melted together with the snow giant. As they woke up, the elves saw only slush and mud outside the window. They grew really homesick and wanted to go home to their sweet native land in their own dense forest.

Impatiently they put on the sponge boots, said goodbye to the host garden, and set off.

Once again the towns and villages flashed by, but this time the travelers never stopped, for the feeling of happiness overwhelmed them as they came closer and closer to their motherland. They quickly passed the fields, forests and cities and reached the border of their country, which they had left three years before.

"Hurrah!" loudly resounded when our forest folk entered their own dear land, and the elves rushed through it faster than the wind. Soon, they passed by the last village and pushed on into the native forest.

Great tears of happiness were in their tiny eyes, their hands hugged their favorite ferns, their tiny mouths kissed each leaf and every blade of the grass.

Soon, our sprites were living the same way as before, remembering in the long winter evenings the warm and cold countries which they visited during their wandering, and always imagining new ventures and new jokes.

About the Book

Book series

The Kingdom of the Elves: Astonishing Adventures around the World includes:

> Book 1: The Elves at the North Pole

> Book 2: From China to India

> Book 3: Welcome to Europe

> Book 4: Long Journey Home

Be sure to look for Books 2-4 of *The Kingdom of the Elves: Astonishing Adventures around the World* on sale in December 2014 and January 2015.

Sign for updates about the series and **FREE EBOOKS** on a launch date at **nyc-books.com**.

History

In 1887, Canadian illustrator Palmer Cox published *The Brownies, Their Book* about imaginary little sprites resembling the popular house spirits of Celtic folklore, who inhabit houses and aid in tasks in return for small gifts of food. Cox's Brownies were little men drawn to represent many professions and nationalities who had mischievous adventures together. This series of humorous verse books and comic strips about kind-hearted pixies soon became incredibly popular and were considered the first commercial comic books, the characters of which were used in advertisements for over 40 companies, including Procter & Gamble and Kodak.

In 1889, the Russian children's writer Anna Khvolson wrote *The Kingdom of the Little Ones: the Astonishing Adventures of the Forest Lilliputians* (Tsarstvo malyutok: udivitelnye priklyucheniya lesnykh chelovechkov). This book was followed by four additional editions in Russia and finally was published in Germany in 1920.

After the breakthrough, the stories about Murzilka (Cox's Dude), the main character of the adventures, and his friends appeared frequently in periodicals. The last known edition in Russia was in 2002.

In *The Kingdom of the Little Ones: the Astonishing Adventures of the Forest Lilliputians*, tiny heroes travel around the world. In the first book, they visit the North Pole and China. In the second, they travel to India, Italy and Switzerland. In the third book, the elves go to Germany, France, England and Holland. Finally, they return home through Germany, Belgium, Austria and Poland. These heroes are endowed with immense curiosity and a passion to discover new and unfamiliar places.

In 2014, Julia Shayk, a lawyer, decided to remake the books for her daughter because both versions of Cox and Khvolson needed editing and corrections to compensate for cultural and social changes of the XXth century. She restructured the text of Anna Khvolson to make the story more coherent; then she translated it into English.

Copyright © 2014 New York Concept

All rights reserved. No part of this book
may be used or reproduced in any manner
whatsoever without a written permission.
For information regarding permission,
please, contact at books@nyc-books.com.

Written by **Anna Khvolson**

Illustrated by **Palmer Cox**

Translated by **Julia Shayk**
(mail.juliashayk@gmail.com)

Edited by **Merrell Knighten**
(editors@doublereadediting.com)

Cover Picture - **Elena Schweitzer**
(http://pi.vu/Bl4V)

Cover Design – **Amandaasia**

For Daniella, Karina,
Mom & Dad, Daniel,
And All The Family
With Love
JS

FROM THE ARROWS OF THE SUN
NOW THE BROWNIE BAND MUST RUN

Let's Connect!

- New releases for either **Free or at $0.99** to all our precious readers during the launch day. To get notified about the launch, *sign up to our mailing list* at **www.nyc-books.com**

- Contact us for any inquiries at **books@nyc-books.com** or **https://twitter.com/nyc_publisher**

- Other books edited, translated or written by Julia Shayk:
www.amazon.com/author/juliashayk or **www.facebook.com/jshayk**

Thank you for purchasing this

New York Concept Book!

Before you go, we'd like to say thank you for purchasing this book. If you find it entertaining and useful, could you, please, take a minute and *leave a review* on amazon.com or other platforms you use to read to rate the book and post your thoughts on Goodreads, Facebook, Twitter, etc?

Your feedback will help us continue to publish books for children and parents.

Also, if you have questions, comments or would like to subscribe to free children tales, young adult stories as well as to parenting tips, please, visit **nyc-books.com**.

72838517R00147

Made in the USA
Lexington, KY
03 December 2017